Top 10 Ways to Kill Your Cast

By
Steve Hudgins

CHAPTER 1

Shall we begin?

So you want to kill your cast, huh?

Okay, let's get right into it. First of all you're going to need a…

Wait a minute…

I have this sneaking suspicion that someone in the cast discovered this book sitting on your chair or on the back of the toilet or wherever you carelessly left it! Which means…they're reading this right now!

Uh oh.

This is not good. Now they know that you want to kill them!

While the thought of murdering one's cast may flash through the minds of many directors, most sane folks won't act on that demented impulse.

You on the other hand took the next step. You bought a book to find out the top 10 ways to kill your cast…and now they know all about it!

I'm no brain surgeon, but I'm pretty sure this kind of thing may be frowned upon. It probably won't put you in their good graces. They may even quit!

That is, IF (notice how big that if is?) IF you are actually plotting to kill your cast, which of course you are not because this is a…uh…joke! Yeah, that's right. This is nothing more than a fun loving innocent joke intended to make your cast laugh and nothing more!

Haha! So what do you think? Isn't this funny?
Wow! The expression on your face!
That was a good one huh?
What a sense of humor your wonderful director has!
There's nothing like a great sense of humor to boost the spirits on the set, that's for sure!
Hell, I think your jolly director deserves a nice big hug and a hearty thank you! Don't you?

LOL!

Well, that was quite the laugh. Okay, now that you know this was just a gag, you can go ahead and put this book down.

I hope you enjoyed the fun. Have a pleasant remainder of your day.

CHAPTER 2

Nothing to see here

It was just a joke, remember?
Nothing to see here.
Just go ahead, put the book down and move along.

CHAPTER 3
Really?

I mean, really? You're still here?

Paranoid much?

The joke is over.

You're actually kind of ruining the jovial mood of it all by continuing to read on.

It's almost as if you don't trust your wonderful, humorous director and let me tell you, that is downright insulting.

How dare you!

Who do you think you are?

This world class director of yours, who happens to have a sense of humor that would make Mel Brooks do a spit take, decides to pull an elaborate prank on you. I say elaborate because they actually purchased this book. That's correct.

They took some of their hard earned money and spent it on this book. Why? To make YOU laugh. To make YOU feel good. And now you have continued reading on well after the joke has been revealed.

Why the persistency? It has been well established at this point that this is a put-on, a lark, a laugh, a clowning. Just some good, old-fashioned tomfoolery.

Yet you're still turning pages. It's as if on the next page you expect to see a list of items one might need to kill you.

Where's the trust?

This is appalling, vile behavior and you should be ashamed of yourself.

Now, for the last time, put this book down and walk away while you still have a shred of decency left.

CHAPTER 4
Ingredients

Here's a list of things you will need in order to kill your cast.

Butcher Knife
Thick Rope or Parachute Cord
Hand Cuffs
Claw Hammer
Rubber Mallet
Bull Whip
Cinder Block
Venus Fly Trap
Paint Thinner
Tweezers
Creepy Doll
Set of 25 Ball Bearings
12 Paper Clips
6 oz Jar of Raspberry Preserves
8 x 10 Autographed Photo of Nick Nolte
Handmade Shawl
Box of Chocolates
Rubber Duck

2 Pairs of Men's Blue Jeans

1 Case of Chalk (Assorted Colors)

2 Pairs of Crotch-less Panties

Water Balloon

Rectal Thermometer

4 Bars of Cocoa Butter Scented Soap

2 Pairs of Used Leg Warmers

Mesh T-Shirt

1 Quart of Heavy Whipping Cream

Dart Board

Wedge Pillow

Garbanzos

Deodorant

3 Bananas

1 Pound of Boysenberries

2 Tampons

Urinal Cake

Pizza Cutter

Flowered Toilet Paper

Baby Powder

1 Pound of Petroleum Jelly

1 Dozen Ostrich Eggs

Lederhosen

Pine Cone

8 ounces of Curry Powder

1 Roll of Fly Paper

CHAPTER 5
The Top 10 List

That lineup of items might seem odd, but it will all make perfect sense once you see the actual list of the top 10 ways to kill your cast.

Without further ado, here is the list…

Oh wait…this isn't you reading this is it? It's that meddlesome cast member again!

Look, you're not going to see the top 10 list, so quit trying.

You do realize this isn't your property, don't you?

Okay, that's it. This chapter is over. As a matter of fact, this entire book is over. You've ruined the fun for everybody! Happy now?
The book stops here.

This is the end.

CHAPTER 6
The book has ended

Did you not read the last sentence of the previous page? The book is over. It's done. Put it down and stop tormenting your godsend of a director!

GOOD BYE!

CHAPTER 7

Go to The Last Page

Okay, this cast member of yours is really annoying! Now I see why you bought this book in the first place!

Hopefully you are reading this chapter before that snoop has. You know what? I'm going to just put the top 10 ways to kill your cast on the last page.

Hurry! Go to the last page. In the meantime, I'll try to keep your irritating cast member preoccupied.

CHAPTER 8
Busted

Yep. I know it's you. The annoying cast member.

Before you go any further, let me share some vitally important information with you.

My name is Steve Hudgins.

I have a series of these types of books that focus on the Top 10 Ways To Kill Your Boss, Cast, Wife, etc. But those aren't the only types of books I write. I also write regular old fiction, typically in the horror and thriller genres.

I have a unique way of writing that is a bit of a screenplay/novel hybrid. It makes for a fast paced read that keeps the descriptive portions of the story simplified which allows the narrative to move along at a swift rate.

You should really check out my author page on Amazon to see all the books I have available.

I also make movies.

I founded Big Biting Pig Productions which is a no-budget production company that specializes in the…you guessed it…horror/thriller genre.

We released ten feature length, no-budget, horror films in nine years. As I write this they're all available to watch for free on Amazon Prime.

You can find out more about the movies at my website: www.bigbitingpigproductions.com

You may be wondering why I'm sharing all this information with you.
Well, I'm going to tell you that, right now…

It was all a distraction!

It was meant to slow you down long enough so that your director could make it to the last page before you!

Ha! Ha!

How does it feel to be outsmarted?

THE LAST PAGE

You found it!

It's the last page.

I had to bury it in the middle of the book to keep your pesky cast from finding it before you did.

So let's get on with the top 10 ways to kill your cast!

Actually, there is no top 10 list.

This really is just a joke.

Assuming your cast has a healthy sense of humor, they should get a good chuckle when they discover this book.

If your cast is filled with a bunch of raging jerks that have a pathetic sense of humor or worse yet, no sense of humor at all, they probably won't find it amusing. They may even be offended. It's possible they will be mad. They may even revolt. In other words, they may act like jerks.

So please, before you attempt this joke, be well aware as to whether or not your cast is super cool or absolute pricks.

CHAPTER 9

Simple ways to use this book

Now that we've established that this entire book is just a harmless gag, let's talk about how to best go about using it.

It's difficult for me to be specific, but the idea is to get your cast to unexpectedly happen upon this book or maybe even discover it as you are actually reading it.

This joke can work with either a paperback or kindle. You probably have a wider variety of options with a paperback but, maybe not! I know there are a ton of creative people out there.

I'd love to see the myriad of ways people are going about letting their cast accidentally, on purpose, stumble across this book and see their reactions!

Post pictures and/or videos on your preferred social media outlet and use the hash tag #top10waystokill

CHAPTER 10

I hope the joke is not on you

That's it. That's all this was ever meant for. Just a laugh.

You didn't really expect to find a legitimate top 10 list detailing ten different ways to murder your cast…did you?

If you did, there is something you should do immediately.

Seek professional help!

And when I say professional help, I don't mean, hire a hit man. I mean find a psychiatrist.
A good one!
Let them know that you are a stark raving lunatic who was seriously considering killing their cast.

Hopefully they'll be able to help you…and I don't mean hopefully they'll be able to help you kill your cast! I mean hopefully they'll be able to help you to not be crazy anymore!

CHAPTER 11

Why are you still here?

Yeah, you saw the title of this chapter.

I know this is the cast member reading again. Seriously, why are you still here?

The jig is up! The cards are on the table! The cat's out of the bag! The whistle has been blown! The beans have been spilled! The skeleton is out of the closet! The pickle has been removed from the jar! The skirt has been raised! The bologna has been exposed! I'm running thin on idioms!

You can go now. Leave. Vamoose. Scoot. Cut out. Take a hike. Vacate. Scram. Blow away. Exit. Split. Clear out. Run along. Push off. Seriously, I have no shortage of synonyms.

I don't understand why you're still reading this. Is it just because there are more pages? The pages in this book are meaningless. They're just padding. I needed some pages in here to make it look like an authentic book.

Are you just going to keep reading the filler? If so, that's kind of pathetic. You may need to reexamine your life.

Wait a minute. You're not still expecting to find a list of ways for someone to kill their cast in here, are you?

I thought I was quite clear about this. I don't know how much more transparent I can be. The list doesn't exist…yet you're still looking because…you want to be sure, don't you?

Oh no, don't tell me…you genuinely suspect that your director may really want to kill you!

CHAPTER 12

So you think your director is a psycho

Okay. Your director has a major screw loose. Here's what you should do…

I don't know.

Why are you expecting me to have the answers?

I wrote this book as a joke. This is meant for a director who has a sick sense of humor and has a good relationship with their cast, who happens to share a similar sick sense of humor.

I wasn't aware that your director wasn't playing with a full deck. I didn't realize their biscuits weren't quite done. I had no idea that their elevator didn't go all the way to the top.

This is scary.

Okay, I'm going to help you. But I have no idea what the current situation is, so I'm going to have to give you instructions based on what I'm imagining.

I picture you on a gigantic, elaborate multi-floor set. This may be the largest set in the history of the world. This particular set is made up to be a colossal mansion. You were about to leave for the night, but had to use the bathroom. You're now sitting on the toilet with your feet propped up on a stool, which is kind of weird. Why the hell are you so comfortable while you're on the toilet? Get up!

In my mind, it's late at night. It's storming. The thunder is deafening!

Your deranged director, who wants to kill you, had already left for the night, but came back to use the toilet themselves. Yes, the very toilet you are standing in front of…or still sitting on if you didn't get up like I told you to!

Now listen to me very carefully. This part is extremely important.

RUN!

Oh wait!

Wash your hands first.

CHAPTER 13

You're running right?

Keep running!

You're running down a long stone corridor that is lined with massive concrete gargoyles. Can you say, creepy?

Jeez, this place is enormous.

Why are all the lights off? Did you turn them off? What were you thinking?

Oh no! What was that sound?

It's a door opening! It sounds like your demented director has entered the corridor…this gargantuan, God-forsaken corridor!

See that closet up ahead? Run to it! Get in there! Shut the door!

Whew. That was close.

Hey, what's that smell? Smells like soap.

Do me a favor and hit the light.

Ugh, I hate those florescent zombie lights that flicker on and off like this one is.

Anyhow, let's gaze around at our surroundings.

Bleach…soap refills…mops….ah, we're in the janitor's closet!

Oooh, what's that over there?

No, the other way! To your right!

Is that a…dirty magazine?

Wow, you were quick to pick that up and start leafing through it!

Are you some kind of pervert?

You do realize you're in a life or death situation don't you?

Hey, what's that smell? It smells like something's burning?

Uh…hello? Yoo hoo. I'm talking to you. Put the magazine down and listen up!

Good.

Now as I was saying, I smell something burning…what in the world is that?

Look over there! It's a wall of lit candles encircling a picture of…you! And another picture of you. And another. And another. Oh and there's one of you getting out of the shower…uh, you didn't know these pictures were being taken, did you?

Oh boy.

So not only do you have an unbalanced nut bar of a director who wants to kill you, but it also appears that the janitor is obsessed with you!

Between you and me, you may want to consider leaving this production.

Okay, we need to get the hell out of this stalker's shrine room.

Place your ear against the door.

Do you hear anything?

Okay good, open the door…

Wait! What are you doing? I was about to say open the door just a crack, I didn't mean for you to push the door all the way open like that! What if that berserker director was standing there! You'd be without a head right now!

Consider yourself lucky. From now on, don't be in such a panic. Keep calm and do what I say.

Next, I want you to run out of this room. And I mean run like Seabiscuit!

Once you're in the corridor, race down to the 2nd floor.

I know what you're thinking. Why the 2nd floor? Why not just dart down to the 1st floor and exit this set? I'll tell you why! Because we're going to outsmart this unhinged whacko!

They're expecting us to go to the 1st floor, so we'll keep one step ahead of them by going to the 2nd floor. From there we'll sneak down the back stairwell to the 1st floor and you'll stealthily peek around to make sure the coast is clear. Then we'll make a mad dash for it!

But first things first! Get to the 2nd floor. I'll meet you there.

CHAPTER 14

The 2ⁿᵈ Floor

What took you so long? I've been waiting here at least 10 minutes! You didn't go back for that magazine did you? Well, it doesn't matter, let's just walk down this corridor and turn the corner…

Ahhh! It's the insane director! And what's that in their hand? A chef's knife!

Here we were thinking we'd be outsmarting them, but in reality we outsmarted ourselves. We should have just gone to the 1ˢᵗ floor!

Oh well, that's all irrelevant now. Hopefully this loony is slow.

Run!

Ooomf! What the hell did we just bump into?

It's the janitor! He's holding a machete…and staring at you with an expression of pure sociopathic love!

Whoa! He just pushed us out of the way and is engaging the screwball director in battle!

This should be a good fight!

I'd love some popcorn as we watch this. Is there a kitchen around here? Oh wait, I suppose since they're both distracted we should take advantage of this moment and flee!

CHAPTER 15
Safety

We're safe now. But that was close!

TOO CLOSE!

Well, I'm sure there is some kind of lesson to be learned here.

Nope.

Not really.

After all, this is just filler.

THE FINAL PAGE

Welcome to the final page.

You were looking for the last page, weren't you?

THE REAL FINAL PAGE

Normally this is where I would put the "about the author" stuff, but I basically did that back in Chapter 8, so I'll just wrap this all up by encouraging you to please join my newsletter at my website: www.bigbitingpigproductions.com Another super cool thing for you to do is follow my Amazon author page.

I hope you had fun!